SOFT SHOULDERS

Written by Liza Frenette

Illustrated by Jane Gillis

SOFT SHOULDERS
An Adirondack Story

Illustrated by Jane Gillis

Second Printing April 2000

*Winner of the Silver Bay Children's Literature Award
sponsored by The Writer's Voice*

ISBN 0-925168-70-X

Library of Congress Cataloging-in-Publication Data

Frenette, Liza, 1958-
    Soft shoulders / by Liza Frenette.
        p.   cm.
        Summary: Ten-year-old Bridget goes out to play on a
snowy day in the Adirondack Mountains and gets lost in a
blizzard with her neighbor Gracey.
        ISBN 0-925168-70-X
        1. Blizzards—Fiction. 2. Lost children—Fiction.
    3. Adirondack Mountains (N.Y.)—Fiction. I. Title.
PZ7.F88935So   1998
[Fic]—dc21   98-35926
                                                         CIP
                                                         AC

North Country Books, Inc.
311 Turner Street
Utica, New York 13501

This book is dedicated to
Jasmine
"M and M"

ACKNOWLEDGEMENTS

Acknowledgements is a big word that means a couple of different things all at the same time. What it means for me is that I want to thank people who helped me be the person who wrote this book.

My grateful thanks go to Katherine Paterson, the talented author of children's books, who chose *Soft Shoulders* as first prize in a national contest and gave me the first spark I needed to believe in my work as a children's author.

To The Writer's Voice chapter in Silver Bay, New York, the organization that sponsored the contest for a children's book set in the Adirondacks, gave me a wonderful prize, recognition, and the incentive to write this.

To Sheila Orlin, former publisher of North Country Books, who believed in this book enough to share its light.

To the naturalists at the Visitors Interpretive Center in Paul Smiths who assisted me with accuracy and information about bogs and plants.

To my writing group, which has been meeting faithfully for several years, Claudia Ricci, Margaret Ervin and Peggy Woods. They help me to draw out my strength as a writer, remind me it's important, and provide me with support, camaraderie and good food.

To Dr. Frederick Smith and Jennifer Oceana Seer, two important people who helped me to heal when I was sick, giving me enough light to write this book. Their kindness and guidance will always be cherished.

To Gerry Colborn, for birds and words.

To friends who have been my community: Linda Hogan (for showing me that I can visualize dreams just like this), Theresa Longhi (for the journal in which I first wrote this book), Darci D'ercole, Cristina Muia, Karen Sleight, Diane Cyr, Jean-Marie Angelo, Charlotte Miller, Rosie Guidice, Linda Lumsden, Linda Hamell, my buddy Jason Carusone, and Lori Martin (who never doubted this would happen and always loves my stories).

To my old friend Beth Gallagher, who shared in the joy of creating this book.

To David Tice, who knew that creating brings life.

To my parents, James and Susanne Hull Frenette, who always made sure I had books, and took me and my eight brothers and sisters on many adventures in the woods. For my brothers Robbie and Michael, especially, who know a lot about taking different paths and the power of both creativity and healing; and for my nieces and nephews, many of whom are in this story, all of whom are in my heart.

To my family, Jasmine, my most important guide.

Contents

Chapter One   *The Snowpants*   Page 1

Chapter Two   *Anna's House*   Page 15

Chapter Three   *Making Plans*   Page 23

Chapter Four   *The Snow Cave*   Page 31

Chapter Five   *The Bogman Wakes Up*   Page 45

Chapter Six   *Burying the Treasure*   Page 61

Chapter Seven   *The Woods at Night*   Page 69

Chapter Eight   *Building a Shelter*   Page 77

Chapter Nine   *Out of the Woods*   Page 87

Chapter Ten   *A Sign*   Page 93

CHAPTER
ONE

The Snowpants

Oh, great. The snowpants. My mom wants me to wear them today to go sledding. I hate wearing those fat, slippery things. They're babyish. And they make me feel like one big lump.

My mom and I argue a lot about the snowpants. I think they're for little kids, like my best friend Anna's sister Gracey, who's five. But I'm ten years old now. That's double her age. But my mother still says I need to wear them to go to school on really cold days, or if I'm going sledding.

I'm supposed to go sledding today with Anna because we have a lot of fresh snow, but after what happened yesterday with the snowpants, I think it might be worth giving up sledding just so I won't have to put on those dreadful squirmy pants again.

NONE of my friends from school have to wear them anymore, except me. Really. But yesterday it was very cold and my mother insisted I wear the snowpants and a wool hat. I cried and everything, but she would not budge. She said I absolutely had to wear them. Positively.

So yesterday morning while I stood waiting for the bus in front of my house I just kept my head down. I was hoping that I could get on the bus really fast and get a seat right behind the driver and no one would notice me. That seemed to be the best I could hope for.

But wouldn't you know, as soon as I clumped my way up the steps to the bus, Mr. Bullock, the bus driver, gave me his usual big smile and said, "Good morning, Bridget! Boy, it's a cold one isn't it! You sure are smart to wear those warm pants."

As he slid the door shut with the big silver handle, I felt my face warming up. I knew it was turning red. Why did he have to say that about my pants? I looked around quickly for a seat.

But I didn't find one soon enough.

Willie, one of my neighbors, stood up and started laughing.

"Oh, look, it's a seal!" he said. "It's a seal out of water!"

Willie's younger brother Charlie was sitting next to him and he started laughing, too. Willie and Charlie could have been twins, they look so much alike. Willie had to start kindergarten a year late because his birthday was just after the deadline for five-year-olds, so he ended up in the same grade as his brother Charlie. The same grade as me, to be exact.

It's bad enough that they live across the field in back of my house, it's bad enough that they both ride my bus, it's bad enough to have ONE of them in my class, but TWO?

And there they were, pointing at me.

"Look everybody! A seal escaped from the zoo!" said Willie.

Charlie, was bouncing up and down in the seat, chanting, "Seal! Seal!" His nose was running, like it usually was, and with each bounce it made it run even more. It was really gross.

I just stood there, glaring at them.

"Boys!" said Mr. Bullock. "That's enough! Leave Bridget alone."

He leaned over to me. "Sorry, Bridget, I didn't mean to embarrass you. Just grab a seat quickly." He gave me a warm smile.

4

Mr. Bullock was really nice.

There were no seats in front of Willie and Charlie, though, so I had to walk by them.

Willie leaned over Charlie, and whispered really loud, "BABY seal, more like it! Because only babies wear snowpants!"

I hissed at him, and then sat at the back of the bus, waiting for Anna and Gracey, who would get picked up next.

It was an awful day. At lunch, Willie and Charlie were at it again, only this time they picked on Anna about her new braces. She's only had them a couple days now, and her lips are all cut and her mouth is still sore. That just gave them more excuses to make fun of her. They called me "Seal," and they called Anna "Steel." Yuck.

And now here was my mom, the very next day, telling me I had to wear the snowpants again. I didn't know if I could stand it. I didn't want to put them on, but I didn't want to stay inside anymore. I was too bored.

I looked at my mother again, to see if maybe she was thinking about changing her mind. But she was on the couch, wrapped up in her quilt, calmly reading a book. I don't even think she was worrying about whether or not I would wear the snowpants. First I just sat and looked at her, the snowpants on the floor in front of me, hoping she would notice my sad face. But she just kept on reading. So I decided to lie down on the floor and make a plan to get out of wearing the snowpants. Maybe she would feel sorry for me, lying on the floor all by myself on a Saturday.

I really wanted to go sledding. I was supposed to spend the day with my dad in town. Usually I see my dad every Saturday and stay overnight with him. But today he had a big test to take to see if he can become a teacher, so I'm home with Mom. My dad and I always go out and get ice cream on Saturday, so ice cream is the next thing on my mind, after the snowpants. I decided it was better to think about ice cream than snowpants, so I started thinking about my favorite flavors, like strawberry swirl, or chocolate marshmallow, or mint chocolate chip....It made me so, so hungry!

At my dad's apartment, we can just walk to a store or an ice cream shop to get ice cream. But out here where I live, on the backside of Whiteface Mountain, you can't walk to any stores. It's even a long way to drive to a store.

My mom says we live in a dip in the mountain. Once she held out her arm in front of her and said, "See the soft spot on the inside of my arm, where it bends at the elbow? That's a hollow, like where we live in the mountain. We live in a nice soft spot called a hollow."

But lying on the floor didn't feel anything like a soft hollow. It felt hard and uncomfortable. It's just that I didn't feel like budging. So I stared at the ceiling and thought about ice cream. The good thing about ice cream is, when you're thinking about it, or eating it, it's really hard to think of anything else. The ice cream is enough.

Since I knew we didn't have any ice cream in the freezer, and since my mom looked so comfortable on the couch, and I knew I wouldn't be able to talk her into going all the way to the store, I decided to try the next best thing.

"Mom, what do you say we bake some chocolate chip cookies?" I said.

She looked up from her book.

"I thought you were going sledding, Bridget," she said.

I didn't answer. She should have known by then that sledding is a problem if I have to wear the snowpants. I even told her about Willie and Charlie, and what they did to me on the bus yesterday, but even though she said she was sorry that happened, she said I'd still have to wear them today because it was so cold out. Besides, she reminded me, Willie and Charlie have karate lessons every Saturday and they wouldn't even be around to see me on the sledding hill where I go with Gracey and Anna.

"Bridget, are you listening?" my mother asked again.

"Yup," I said.

"Well, I don't think I can start baking cookies right now, because with the way it's snowing so hard, I'm sure I'm going to get called in to work any minute. In fact, I'm surprised they haven't called already."

My mom usually has to work whenever it snows really hard. You see, my mom works for the Department of Transportation. Everyone calls it D-O-T; you know they spell it out as if they're just learning to read or something. But I think that's babyish. So I call it DOT. I squish all the letters together and call it just plain old DOT. It sounds friendlier that way.

8

My mom rides in a big yellow snowplow. We get a lot of snow here in the Adirondack Mountains where we live, and my mom helps to keep the roads clear in the winter so that it's safe to drive. She has to work a lot, because it snows a lot around here. Then in the summer, when there's no snow, she has a lot of time to spend with me when I'm out of school.

What my mom does is she sits up high in this giant yellow truck and she lifts the wing plow on the side of the truck up and down to clear the sides of the road from any snow. She leaves really big snowbanks behind her. Her work partner drives and lifts the plow in the front of the truck while my mom takes care of the side plow. Together they clear one whole side of the road of snow, and then they turn around and plow the other side.

Her partner in the truck used to be my dad, but now he works somewhere else, because he needed a job with regular hours, not like snowplowing. That's because he goes to college at night now, where he's studying to become a high school teacher. The college is at least a one hour drive each way, and then my dad has classes that last three hours. So he's pretty busy. I thought about how my father has to drive an hour each way to college three or four nights a week, and some of the roads he drives on have been plowed by my mother.

My dad lives about a half hour from us in a little town called Saranac Lake, because he and my mom are divorced, which is something I don't quite understand. I'd rather think about how they met, which was driving the plow together on a snowy night.

My mom and I don't really live in a town. There's just houses scattered here and there on the backside of the mountain. We don't even have our own store or post office. And we definitely don't have any ice cream. Which reminded me that I was still hungry, and I was still lying on the floor. And my mom was still reading her book, not noticing me.

"Well, if you're not going to make cookies with me, then what am I supposed to do?" I asked my mom. "It's not fair."

She looked over the top of her book.

"You could go sledding," she said. "Gracey and Anna are probably waiting for you. You said you'd be over by now. Just put the snowpants on. Do we have to have this discussion every time it's really cold out?"

I don't know why she calls it a discussion. I think it's a good, old-fashioned argument. And I think I'd like to win once in a while.

"The snowpants are too warm, Mom. I'll get too hot going up the hill all those times," I said. "I'll suffocate!"

She put her head to one side, like she's getting ready to sigh.

"Bridget, sometimes you tire me out you know," she said kind of loudly. I guess that meant she was getting mad.

I just lay still on the floor. I wondered if she knew that she tired me out too. Maybe she would realize I was so tired out I couldn't get up, and then she'd see that I should win this argument. I stared at the ceiling. I blinked a lot. Maybe I would be here on the floor so long that I'd get weak from hunger and then she'd feel really bad she ever

11

made a stink about snowpants. I waited. She didn't say anything.

"Dad never makes me wear them!" I said suddenly. "And today's Saturday, and I usually spend Saturday with Daddy, so it should be okay not to wear them, because it's Saturday. And besides, I didn't get any ice cream, so I should get a break."

Then my mom let out her long sigh. She does this a lot when she runs out of energy. I looked over at her, hopeful that she'd finally seen my point.

She lifted up her quilt and motioned for me to come sit next to her on the couch.

Slowly, I got up off the floor, hanging my head down. My big wool socks slid across the hardwood floor, though, and this made me laugh. I sat next to my mom and scooched under her arm—there's always a warm spot there—and she settled the quilt over my knees.

I love looking at my mother's quilt. She made it herself, and it's full of squares of material all patched together into designs of trees. Some of the patches are from my old clothes, and I remember wearing them when I was little. Each tree has its own square. This is how I learned to name the trees that I see every day: birch, white pine, oak, maple, balsam, red pine, spruce, hemlock, and tamarack. Each tree is different, and they all grow here in the Adirondacks. Every square is hooked together with tiny, neat, white stitches that are so small I have to squint to see them. They look like my baby teeth that I used to leave out for the tooth fairy.

"Bridget," said my mom. "Your dad doesn't make you wear

snowpants because you don't go sledding when you're with him. You go sledding out here, with Anna and Gracey. No one even sees you."

"No one even sees me because practically no one else lives out here," I said.

"But there's a lot of wonderful things to do out here, and you know how much you love them. Like cross-country skiing, and making forts in the forest, and sledding. It's pretty here," she said.

"But Mom, the thing is that the snowpants make me look like a baby. And I'm not a baby anymore. I'm nearly grown up. I want to be a babysitter soon, Mom. And no one's going to take me seriously if they know I still have to wear snowpants. Next year I want to take the babysitting class at the library in Saranac Lake so I can learn to be a babysitter. And I need to be serious!"

At first my mother started laughing, but I gave her my serious look—I do this by flattening my eyebrows—and then she stopped.

"You'll be a good babysitter some day, Bridget, no matter what you wear today. But today I want you to be warm. It's very cold. If you wear the snowpants, you'll be able to stay out longer."

Just then the phone rang, and my mom climbed out of the couch and went to answer it in the kitchen.

"Hello? Oh, yes, I figured you'd be calling. Okay, I'll be there soon," she said, and hung up.

She looked at me and we both rolled our eyes.

"Time to go to work!" we both said at the same time.

My mom came over and gave me a hug.

"Bridget, how about if I bring you home some ice cream when I come home from work?" she asked.

I looked up at her and smiled.

"It's a deal," I said.

CHAPTER TWO

Anna's House

My mom and I held each other's mittens while we walked to Anna's house. I go to Anna's house whenever my mother has to go to work at funny hours. Then in the summer, when my mom is home a lot, she watches Anna and Gracey for their parents. It's a good deal, because each way I get to spend a lot of time with my friends.

I stuck my tongue out to see if I could catch any snow, but the soft flakes mostly brushed my sky-pointed cheeks.

I like the snow best when it's soft. I don't like corn snow very much; that's when the snow is kind of hard and wet and grainy at the same time. I like it when the snow just seems to come down packy because that's when Anna and Gracey and I make big snowmen.

Well, except that since we're girls, what we usually make is a snowLADY. We just sort of decided one day that it would be nice to see some snowladies instead of just snowmen all the time. Or sometimes we make a man and a lady.

When we make a lady, we walk to the bog behind the big field in back of our houses and get some dried moss. We use this to make curly hair-dos. One time we stuck in short little pine branches to make a spiked hair-do like I've seen older girls in magazines wear. Then we brought out one of my dress-up gowns and put it on the snowlady. It was kind of hard getting it over her head because of all the branch hair. But we did it. Except that once we got the dress over the snowlady, it sagged.

We stood there looking at it a long time. Then we both sort of figured out at the same time what was missing. So then we went and found two rocks and put them in the top part of the dress, because really Anna and I wanted to see what it would look like if you didn't have any breasts, and then suddenly you did. Like us—someday.

It was pretty hard to find two rocks the same size, but we got as close as we could to matching them up. We stuck them underneath the dress, pushing them into the snow so they would stick, and then stood back to see how it looked. And really, it looked sort of lopsided.

So we started giggling, and we promised not to tell anyone, ever, what we'd done because it was so silly. But then one rock slipped down and it got stuck in the belt! And the other rock was up there by itself! By then it was so funny that we just had to tell SOMEBODY. We each told our moms, and they laughed, too.

"Maybe after we go sledding today Anna and I will build a snowlady," I told my mom. "Do you think the snow is packy enough today?"

"I think so," my mom said.

"I hope you get home early so I can sleep in my own bed and maybe even have pancakes tomorrow," I said.

"I hope so, too," my mom said.

Whenever she has to work late in the winter, I sleep at Anna's. Sometimes I even have to go to Anna's in the middle of the night, if it starts snowing heavily all of a sudden and they need my mom to come plow. I don't really like waking up at night and getting in another bed that's not warm from me yet. Neither does my bear Lester. But I do like sleeping in the same room with my friend. That part is nice. And

if it's a weeknight, we get to wait for the bus together and everything the next morning. It's like having a sometime sister. My mom said sometimes you can make your own family bigger with friends. She said sometimes friends can be just the family you need.

I remember one of the first times that I stayed over at Anna's late at night. I lay in bed for a long, long time. I could hear Anna's breathing, but it didn't make me sleepy at all. I just felt very strange not having my mother or father sleeping somewhere else down the hall. I tried to think of all kinds of good things, like about my favorite foods and my favorite books, but I still couldn't fill up my mind with enough good stuff to get to sleep. I felt my eyes fill with water, and then I knew I was crying even though I was trying to think about mashed potatoes with a lot of butter, which I love.

Then through my tears I saw the quick splash of a yellowish light on the wall. I turned over to look at the bedroom door, thinking maybe Anna's mom had opened the door to check on us and the hallway light had spilled in. But the door was shut. Then I saw another flash of yellow.

I got out of bed and went over to the window, and down the road I could see it was the swirling yellow light that was on top of the big snowplow my mother drove. The light is always on when the snowplow is on the road because the snowplow moves slowly and sometimes it's hard for people driving down the road to see it ahead of them if it's snowing really hard. The yellow light can be seen even through a really heavy snowfall, so it warns other drivers. And I could sure see the bright yellow light that night. I pressed my face to the cold window.

Then, as the snowplow got closer, I could hear the scraping sounds of the two plows. I felt a big smile spread across my face. It seemed like it spread all the way through me and right down to my toes, which should have been cold because I was barefoot on the floor. But I was warm as could be, because there was my mom out plowing the roads and keeping us all safe. And even though I know she couldn't see me because the house was dark, I saw her look up real quick when the truck passed by, and I know she was thinking about me. After that I fell right to sleep.

CHAPTER
THREE

Making Plans

Most of the time I sleep at Anna's now it's real easy. I know my mom is out there plowing and that she'll be home soon. If it weren't for her plowing, the school buses wouldn't be able to get to our house. We wouldn't be able to drive to the store to get food! Or go to the movies! My dad wouldn't be able to come get me, either. All the roads would be blocked.

I'm pretty used to staying at Anna's now during big snowstorms. Sometimes I go for dinner, and it's just like I'm part of their family. I even have chores to do, which isn't so great, but I'd have to do them at my house anyway, so I guess it's okay.

I do my homework in the living room after dinner, and Anna and I can help each other because we're in the same grade. It makes the homework less like a chore that way. When it's bedtime, her dad usually comes in to say goodnight in the doorway while her mom tucks me in. And sometimes that makes me get a little lump in my throat.

You see, Anna's dad doesn't have a mustache, and when I see him in the doorway I always think about my dad's mustache and how it tickles me when he kisses me goodnight. And that makes me miss my dad a lot and wish I could see him every day. That's when I hug Lester extra hard. My dad gave me Lester.

"Lester can be with you when I can't," he said when he gave the bear to me.

Even though my dad doesn't live with us anymore, he calls me every single day, and sometimes he picks me up from school and we have dinner together at his apartment, if it's a night that he doesn't have to go to college. Then he brings me back out here. Plus I stay overnight every Saturday with him in Saranac Lake.

Well, every Saturday except this one, I guess.

Usually on Saturday afternoons we go to the library near his house before we go out for ice cream. The library is where I saw the sign for the babysitter course. It said that you have to be eleven years old to take the course. So I'm going to sign up next year, when I'm eleven. Then I can be a babysitter.

My dad said he'd take me to the course next year, even though it's on school nights. "No problem," he said. He's nearly done with college, and pretty soon he'll have more time. He said he'd come out and pick me up after school and take me into Saranac Lake on the nights I wanted to take the course.

It's a really pretty ride from my mom's house to my dad's. All you have to do is ride down the rest of the Whiteface Mountain road, where we live, past a little town called Bloomingdale, and then there's just a couple of miles of long, flat fields with some cows before you get into Saranac Lake.

I think the fields look like they've been swept clean by the wind, and then all of the swept-up piles were left at the end of every field, until there were so many piles on top of each other they became mountains. Because every way you turn your head, there's mountains at the edge of the field. They're beautiful.

That's just how it is here in the Adirondacks.

When we drive, Dad tells these really neat stories about road signs. I'm pretty sure he makes them up, but sometimes it's hard to tell.

First there's always the big yellow sign that says SOFT SHOULDERS. My dad says that means that it's okay to pull over and cry if you need to because everyone has a soft shoulder to lean on, even if they don't always see it. And the sign is just a reminder of that, he says.

There's also this other sign that says SLIPPERY WHEN WET. My dad says it's a sign to let the raccoons know that this is a good spot for ice skating. Raccoons have padded paws that are just right for skating, he said. It does make sense.

When we get to the STOP sign in Bloomingdale, my dad always quizzes me.

"What does that one mean, Bridget?" he asks.

"Slow Tourists On Parade," I say, and then he laughs. STOP is the first letter of each word in Slow Tourists on Parade. We get a lot of tourists here in the Adirondacks because it's so pretty, and people come here to hike and ski, and my dad says you can always tell the tourists because they drive slow and look at everything and smile a lot, just like people in a parade.

I love my dad's stories about the road signs. It makes me smile when I think about them, like now.

Suddenly, I tugged my mother's mitten.

"What is it, Bridget?" she asked. We were almost to Anna's

house, but I needed her to stop.

"Mom, you know how Dad tells those stories about the road signs?" I said.

"Yes," she said, smiling.

"Well, I just thought of one myself!" I said. "You know how every once in awhile you see a road sign that says FALLEN ROCK ZONE? Well, I could never figure out what that meant, as if rocks would be falling from the sky or something. I mean that's pretty stupid. But now I know what it really means. You know how I was telling you how I might make a snowlady today? Well, remember the snowlady that Anna and I made, and we put those rocks in her dress but one fell into her belt? Well, guess what, she had a fallen rock! So the sign on the road that says FALLEN ROCK ZONE means you should watch out for snowladies with fallen rocks!"

My mother put her mitten over her mouth because she was laughing so hard. And I started laughing, too.

By now we were at Anna's house, and I stood on my tiptoes to kiss my mother good-bye. She said she'd try to get home early. Then she bent over and whispered our secret word right into my ear. Then I whispered it back into hers. Only she and I know the word. It's made up. I never even told Anna.

"I love you," I said.

"I love you, too," she said, and then she waved and walked back home so she could go to work.

I went inside and Gracey and Anna were already waiting for

me. I let out a big breath of relief when I saw that Anna had on snow-pants just like mine.

Our mothers must have planned this on the phone.

Gracey had a snowSUIT—you know, the whole, one-piece thing. I was so glad I didn't have to wear those anymore. It made me feel a little bit bigger. At least mine were just the pants.

Anna pulled me over to her side right away.

"My mother's making us take Gracey along for the WHOLE afternoon," she said through her cut lips. "How are we ever going to do our secret plan with her along?"

I'd been so worried about the snowpants and my hunger for ice cream that I'd nearly forgotten about the plan. We came up with the idea yesterday after school while we were waiting for the bus to come. We had a plan to get back at Willie and Charlie for picking on us.

"Well," I whispered, "Why don't we take her sledding and maybe she'll just get tired out after that and then one of us can bring her back to the house. Then whoever brings her back can get the stuff we need off my back porch. Don't worry, Anna. This will work."

"What are you guys talking about?" asked Gracey, tugging at my jacket.

"Just school stuff," I told Gracey. That was kind of the truth. Everything had started in school. I leaned down and gave her a hug.

"Come on, let's go sledding!" I said. Gracey clapped her hands and Anna and I winked at each other. We had a good plan. I couldn't wait to trick Willie and Charlie.

The three of us went outside, and as we kicked our way across the field, shoving the toes of our boots into the snow, we told Gracey that we'd have some sledding races today.

First, though, Gracey wanted to stop and make snow angels. The snow falling today left a new, fresh layer of pure white powder, and it was perfect for making angels. We spread apart, and then we each fell backward, laughing, into the snow.

I spread my arms and legs as wide as they would go, up and down, back and forth, again and again, to make the angel's wings and her skirt. My arms and legs made a soft noise in the snow as they moved, like a shh, shh, shh sound.

"Hey, I'm a windshield wiper!" Gracey said as she moved her arms back and forth. We all laughed.

I looked up at the beautiful blue sky and thought that it was a perfect day for an angel. I thought that I would name my angel Jasmine, which is the name of a girl I met one time last summer at the beach when my mother took just me and her to Cape Cod for a couple of days. Jasmine and I played in the waves together, and it was a lot of fun having a friend, because I'd never been swimming in the ocean before and I wasn't used to the big, salty waves. I thought her name was so beautiful and special, like a mermaid's name or something, because Jasmine just seemed to sort of appear in the waves while I was swimming. I'd never heard that name before. She told me she was named after a little white flower that grows on a plant and smells beautiful. I looked it up in the plant book my mother has when I got home, but the jasmine flower isn't a native plant of the Adirondacks.

I stood up carefully and then stepped away to look at my angel. She was so pretty.

"My angel's name is Jasmine," I said to Gracey and Anna. "She's going to be my guardian angel."

"What kind of angel is that?" Gracey asked.

"A guardian angel is someone who watches over you, " I said, "even though you can't always see them."

"Oh," she said. "I like that idea. I'm going to name my angel Patty after my doll-baby," Gracey said, and she turned around and showed me her doll-baby who was riding along in the hood of her snowsuit.

"That's a nice name," I said.

"Did you bring Lester with you today?" she asked me.

"Yup," I said, and turned to show her my bear, who was in the hood of my jacket. We laughed.

"I'm going to name my angel Sparkle," Anna said. "Because when I finally get my braces off, my teeth will sparkle like an angel's teeth."

We said good-bye to our angels, and walked off toward the sledding hill. Gracey was a little bit slower, so while she walked behind us, Anna and I went over our plans. Yesterday, while we had waited for the bus after school, we drew a fake treasure map with a bunch of clues. The clues would lead someone to a wooded area with a bunch of birch trees beyond the big field between our house and the

34

back of Willie and Charlie's house. We wrote the words "Birthday Money" in tiny letters in the place where the secret treasure would be found, so they'd think we were burying the money we'd gotten for our birthdays in a secret spot.

Then we crumpled up the map, and when I got off the bus at my house, I pretended that I dropped it in the aisle and didn't notice. We knew that Willie and Charlie would pick it up when they got off at the next stop. They were always snooping for something of ours that they could pick on us about. On the top of the map we'd put in big letters, TOP SECRET TREASURE HUNT FOR SATURDAY.

Of course, we weren't really going to bury our birthday money, like they would think we would. Instead, we were going to get a metal pail, which my mother kept on the back porch. It was always filled with old food and leftovers and yucky stuff that my mother saved for the compost pile. She used all this stuff to make compost so the soil would be better for her garden in the summer.

Last night I also left out some milk on the counter, behind the breadbox so my mother wouldn't find it, so it would spoil. Just before we took the pail out to bury it we were going to dump the spoiled milk over everything.

And when Willie and Charlie dug up that bucket, it would smell! And they'd get their hands all dirty and slimy, too, digging for the money! That would show them they should leave us alone!

"I only wish I could be there to see their faces when they open up that pail!" Anna said. "Boy, would that be great fun to secretly watch them!"

"Yeah!" I agreed.

"Hey, there's our sleds!" shouted Gracey.

Sure enough, there were our sleds, propped up against a tree. We always left them back there near the sledding hill. We each had a different color. Mine was green and Gracey's was orange and Anna's was yellow. They looked like big, bright cold popsicles.

The big hill was smooth and fast as ever. We climbed up and slid down again and again, walking back up the hill, swish, swish, swishing our snowpants as our legs rubbed together with each step. We squealed whenever we landed at the bottom, waiting for the snow to spray us.

On one trip Gracey put Patty on her sled, and I put Lester next to the doll, and we pushed them down the hill together. Gracey and I laughed because they flopped all over each other and got covered with snow.

The three of us had some sledding races, too. Anna was usually the fastest. Then Gracey and I decided to go in the sled together a couple times. She liked sitting in my lap.

But then I noticed that Anna was getting bored or something. I can always tell this because she starts clicking her tongue against the back of her front teeth when she's antsy. Then she started shuffling around in the snow, kicking her feet, looking away from us. I guess she wanted to start the treasure hunt, but we didn't dare do it with Gracey around. It had to be secret.

Suddenly Anna started waving her arms. "Hey, look you guys!" she said, pointing.

I squinted. At the edge of the field, hidden in the shadow of a cliff, was one of the new hideouts we had made late in the fall. An overhang off the cliff was just like a roof, and the cliff itself made one wall. We'd made another side wall and a back wall with pine boughs that had fallen from nearby trees. I'd cut them to the right length with my Swiss Army knife that my father had given me for my last birthday. The front of the cave was open so we could see out. And now, the whole thing was completely covered with snow!

"We can make it our secret snow cave!" Anna said. "We never had a snow cave before!"

"This is going to be great!" I hollered to her. "Come on, Gracey, let's go!"

We ran over to the cave. It was beautiful inside, so quiet and so private. It could be our winter house!

I found a couple of small rocks beneath some snow, and we rolled them inside so that we'd have seats. Then Anna and I found some fallen bark near the trunks of some trees. We could pretend it was dishes for our house. Gracey found a bunch of pine needles and made a broom out of them to sweep out the cave.

"Look," she said, "I'm helping."

"Good job," Anna told Gracey, giving her a hug. "Now we all have a secret place to go in the winter."

"Yeah," said Gracey, whispering, "And I won't tell anybody."

She moved her hand like she was turning a key in her lips, and then threw away the pretend key.

When we finally all sat down inside the space, it was kind of crowded. We sat on our rocks, our knees nearly touching. We could look out and see the mountains. We were safe from the falling snow. We were in a secret house, and no one could tell us to pick up after ourselves.

"Let's make a rule," I said, "that we can be as messy as we want in our house and we never have to clean up."

Gracey and Anna agreed.

"If only we had some food," I said. "Next time we come out here we could bring some food and have a winter picnic."

Inside the hideout, our breath was smoky and warm. Hmmm.... I smelled something familiar. I smelled...chocolate! I turned to the left and sniffed, and then to the right.

"Gracey, do you have chocolate?" I asked.

"I have some chocolate chip cookies," she said, smiling, and reached into her pocket and pulled out a little plastic bag filled with crumbled chunks of cookies.

"EW!" said Anna. "They're gross!"

"SO?" said Gracey.

"I'll eat some," I said, and took off my mittens. Chocolate was chocolate. I didn't care if it was broken into pieces. The cookies were pretty soggy, though, and they stuck to my teeth. I curled up my lip and smiled at Anna.

"That's gross," she said, wrinkling her nose.

Then she turned to her sister.

"Gracey, I think I better take you home now. It's time for your nap."

Gracey shook her head "No," and stuck out her tongue, which was filled with mushy crumbs and cookie goo.

"I'm telling Mom you took treats without asking," Anna said.

Gracey's lower lip came out, and I knew she'd start crying any minute. She cries REALLY loud. I had to think quickly, because she was so close to my ears.

"Hey, Gracey, before Anna takes you home, how about we go to the bog first, and maybe we can find some pitcher plants under the snow?" I said. "We could bring them back and pretend to have tea in them. Then we could have a little tea party with cookies and then you could go take your nap, okay?"

Gracey's face brightened.

"I never saw pitcher plants before," she said. "Are they pretty?"

"They're very pretty," I said.

"Okay!" she said. "It'd be fun to see plants in the winter."

"I'm not going," said Anna.

She cupped her hand to my ear and whispered, impatiently, "We have to get the stuff buried before Willie and Charlie get back from karate!"

I thought we still had a lot of time. But I know Anna worries a lot. And maybe she was mad about me spending more time with

Gracey. Or maybe she was just tired of having her little sister around all day. Or maybe her braces hurt a lot today.

Anna turned toward Gracey, her eyes really narrow like the eyes of the salamander I caught once.

"Bridget came to play with ME today," she said. "Why don't you go watch Sesame Street or something?"

That did it. Gracey started crying loudly. In the small snow cave, it sounded like someone crying into headphones that were stuck in my ears. I wasn't sure what to do. I noticed that I was becoming hot in my snowpants. I didn't want Anna to get mad at me. She's my best friend. And I sure didn't want Gracey crying in my ears.

No one said a word, and Gracey started crying even louder, stopping and starting between gasps. She sounded kind of like the alarm at school when there's a fire drill.

I thought if I was going to be a babysitter some day, I better learn what to do when a kid starts crying. I looked over at Gracey. Her face was smeared with chocolate and her nose was running. She wiped it with her mitten and it smeared everything on her face even more. I could barf!

I put my head between my knees. Then I had an idea. I whispered to Anna and told her to go back to my house and get the stuff off the back porch, plus the sour milk, while I took Gracey to the bog. Then we'd all meet back here at the snow cave and have our little pretend tea party.

After that, I could walk Gracey back home while Anna got

42

started on the plan. She would have to tie yarn around some trees on the way to the hiding spot to mark them the way the map showed.

By the time she was done doing that, I'd be back from walking Gracey home, and we could bury the treasure together.

At first Anna just sat there with her arms folded. I guess sometimes its hard having a little brother or sister to take care of. I really don't know.

"Okay," she said finally. "That's a good plan."

"Did you remember the yarn?" I asked.

She opened her pocket and showed me different colored yarn all wrapped up. It looked like a spiderweb that had been all colored in with crayons.

"What are you guys talking about and looking at?" Gracey asked, her lower lip stuck out in a pout.

"Just never mind," Anna said.

"Come on, Gracey, let's go to the bog!" I said, pulling her up from the rock. I didn't want Gracey to get upset again.

CHAPTER
FIVE

The Bogman
Wakes Up

While Gracey and I walked to the bog, swish, swish, swishing in our snowpants, she kept hiccuping from crying.

I told her that I'd tell her some stories. She liked that idea. So I told her all about the road signs that my father had taught me. I told her how SOFT SHOULDERS was a sign to remind you that you would always have a shoulder to cuddle up to and cry on when you were feeling sad, like your mom's or dad's shoulder, even if they weren't there right that minute.

"Or like the guardian angels you told me about today," Gracey said. "They could have a soft shoulder to cry on too, right? The snow angel you made looked like she had shoulders."

"That's right, Gracey," I said. "You're very smart."

And I told her about the sign that said SLIPPERY WHEN WET, and she liked the idea of raccoons going skating.

"I like to skate, too!" she said. "I hope I see them out skating sometime when I am!"

She said she liked that sign the best. I told her how much fun she was going to have when she learned to read. She said she was doing one letter book a week in kindergarten, and she was already up to the letter J.

By the time I'd finished telling Gracey about all my favorite signs, we'd reached the bog. It was a pretty long walk, but I knew the way really well, past the big meadow, through some paths in the forest, and then out to the open area of the bog.

It was real quiet there. The wind was lifting up snow from the frozen water in the bog and pushing it across the ice. It looked like white, lacy scarves blowing in the wind.

Gracey said the snow on the bog looked like "whitehats."

"Whitehats?" I asked. "What do you mean?"

"Like at the ocean," she said. "One time me and Anna and my mom and dad all went to the ocean. You know, like where you went, that time you met that girl Jasmine. Hey, Jasmine, that's a letter J! That's my letter this week!"

"That's right, that's the letter. And I know what you meant by whitehats. You mean whiteCAPS," I said, laughing. "You're right. That's what they look like."

It was a nice way to think of the bog, since a lot of the water is actually covered with that spongy spaghnum moss. I know this from a book we read in science class.

We bent our heads down and scuffed our toes along the edges of the bog, trying to find some treasures for our snow cave tea party. I found a few small, pretty stones underneath the snow. We could pretend they were cookies.

"Look!" Gracey said.

I went over to where she was squatting on the ground. There, in a pile of snow, was a bunch of purple and green pitcher plants.

"That's them!" I said. "Those are pitcher plants!"

"How do they live in winter?" Gracey asked, frowning.

"They have real hard leaves," I said. "My dad told me that helps them live in cold weather. I knew they grew near this bog, but

this is the first time I've seen them in winter. They're really beautiful."

"Yeah, they are," Gracey said. "What do they eat in winter?"

"I don't know. I'll have to ask my dad," I said. "But I know in the summer they trap insects inside their leaves, like mosquitoes and flies, for food."

"I'm glad they eat them," Gracey said. "I can't stand mosquitoes." Then she wrinkled her forehead as she thought.

"Bridget, maybe we should leave them instead of picking them. I want there to be A LOT of pitcher plants to eat ALL the mosquitoes next summer!"

I smiled at her.

"That's a good idea. My dad says it's smart to leave plants for others to see, anyway. We'll just come back and check on them sometimes," I said.

"Yeah, and it will be our secret. And then we'll have a secret hideout in the winter and secret plants that no one else knows where they are," she said in a whisper.

Just then I thought I heard a voice calling from far away. I looked into the sky. It was snowing hard, and the wind was blowing even harder. I listened again, but I didn't hear anything. It must have been my imagination.

I noticed though, that the sky seemed a little darker, like the light above us had gotten squished or something.

"Come on, Gracey," I said, taking her hand and pulling her up.

"We have to go meet Anna back at the snow cave now."

I brushed off her hat. It was covered with snow.

"It sure is snowing a lot today," I said.

We walked around the bog, and then past the circle of tamaracks, which I know because they lose their needles in the winter, and they can grow near a bog.

My mom says it's unusual for a tree to grow near a bog, because a bog has no oxygen. I know about the tamarack because it's the last square in my mother's quilt, and she made the needles a burnt gold color, just the color that they are before they drop off the tree. I shivered, wishing I was under my mother's quilt right now.

We passed through another patch of trees and I started thinking about how we would dig a hole to bury our secret treasure. It would be pretty tough to dig in the dirt because the ground was really hard this time of year. I knew for sure that at least the top of the ground would be frozen. We hadn't even thought about that. I hoped our plan wasn't ruined. We'd never be able to dig with just our hands.

I was so busy worrying about the plan that I guess I didn't notice where we were going, even though we've been back to the bog a million times. It was snowing pretty hard when we came out of the woods, and I wasn't sure if we were going the right way. I looked down to see if I could find our footprints, but the wind had blown snow over our tracks.

Suddenly Gracey tugged at my sleeve.

"I left my doll-baby back at the snow cave!" she said. "She'll be afraid."

"You know what?" I said. "I left Lester there too. Lester will take care of her. Don't worry."

I tucked my arm in hers and we started walking. The tips of my toes were starting to get a little bit cold, and if I lifted my face up it got too cold in the wind. So I kept looking to the side to find markings. And then I got so mad I stamped my foot! We were back at the bog again! We had just walked in a circle.

And now the bog looked kind of dark and swirly. I looked up and the sky was filled with really big storm clouds.

Then I heard a couple of loud, rumbling noises. They were like burp sounds deep beneath the ice. I tried to tell myself it was just ice forming. I'd heard it many times. But now, in the snow and the grayness, it sounded so deep and scary.

At first, Gracey laughed.

"Hey, it's a burp!" she said. "My friend Peter can burp really loud like that. He's in my class at kindergarten. Every time he burps he laughs. But the teacher doesn't like it that much."

"That's a loud noise," I said. "I can't believe your friend can burp that loud."

But as I stood in the snow, listening to the growling, I remembered this video Anna and I had seen with our class on a field trip to the educational nature center in Paul Smiths.

The video told a true story about a man who was thousands of years old who had been found in a bog in England. His body was still

52

like new after all that time! It hadn't rotted away like most dead things do after awhile, because the bog didn't have any air to eat away his body. The bog kept him fresh.

They called him "The Bogman."

He was in such good shape when they found him, that his last meals were still in his stomach. Gross! And now here we were, hearing burps near a bog. Maybe those burps were real. Maybe there was a Bogman right here in the Adirondack Mountains and he was waking up with a really bad stomach ache from thousand-year-old food sitting in his belly.

Maybe this Bogman was in such good shape that he was still alive, only he'd be all smelly and mean from a stomach ache.

I wondered if he smelled Gracey's chocolate chip cookie crumbs. Or if he smelled us, and it woke him up.

The ice growled again. The wind started blowing harder, and it seemed to make a shrieking sound. Gracey held my hand a little bit tighter.

"I'm scared, Bridget," she said.

"It's just the sound of the ice," I said.

"But why are we back here at the bog?" Gracey asked. "I thought we were going to the snow cave to get Lester and Patty and then go home."

"I got a little mixed up walking home," I said. "I guess I was daydreaming. Come on, we'll go back now."

"Good," she said. "I'm getting kinda' hungry. And my friend

Peter is going to come over for supper tonight. My mom said that since Anna has a friend over—that's you—that I could have one too. We're going to have spaghetti."

"That will be fun, Gracey," I said. I leaned down and tucked her scarf around her face to keep the wind off her. I was glad she didn't know about The Bogman. I wondered if he was watching us.

As soon as we turned to go back home, a big wind sent the snow swirling everywhere. Gracey put her head down to block the snow. There was another loud growling sound.

"Uh oh, my boot is untied," she said. "But I know how to tie it all by myself now."

Gracey bent down to tie her boot and while I waited for her, I thought I saw something moving through the snow. I put my hand over my eyes to block some of the snow so I could see better. It was too big for an animal. It was...yes, it was...a shape...like a ghost or something...

It was full of shadows, but as it slowly stepped closer I was pretty sure I could make out a face in the blowing snow. Yes, it was a face all twisted up. Oh, no...it must be The Bogman! Those burps must have been real! It was coming toward us, and I could see that it had something in its hand.

My heart started pounding. It was walking toward us, all blurry in the snow and the shadows of late afternoon. It looked mean. I heard another shriek, and I realized that what I had thought was the wind must have been The Bogman screaming. I could see pieces of hair

around its face, and it looked like it had on some kind of hood. Snow was blowing everywhere, and I didn't know which way to turn. I felt frozen in place.

I have never been so scared in all of my life. It looked worse than any Halloween outfit I've ever seen on dark nights when I was trick-or-treating. I wished I was dreaming.

It was getting closer, and I started backing up slowly, and then it lifted something over its head. It was a sword, I thought! It was The Bogman with an old sword! It was coming to get us!

Gracey stood up.

"Run!" I said, grabbing her hand.

"Why?" she asked.

"Run to stay warm! Come on, it will keep us warm!" I didn't want to scare her, but we needed to move. Fast. We both turned and started running. The snow pelted down on our faces. I could feel my heart pounding all the way through my undershirt, my turtleneck, my sweater, and my jacket. It felt like my heart was outside my jacket.

I head another shriek, then a voice calling, and I thought, "Oh no, it can talk!" The voice got louder.

"WAIT!" it said.

I ran faster.

"WAIT! It's me. It's ANNA!"

Gracey and I both stopped. We looked at each other.

We turned around slowly.

The figure came closer. I took a couple steps backward. But

sure enough, as she got closer and the shadows disappeared from her face, I could see it was Anna.

I've been happy to see Anna many times in my life, but this was definitely the happiest.

"Hey, slow down," she hollered, huffing from being out of breath. "Look what I found on your back porch! A shovel!" She was holding it over her head. "We can use it to dig for the treasure! We would never have been able to bury anything with just our hands. The ground is too hard. I was glad when I saw the shovel."

I felt my heart start to slow down. Maybe it would go back inside my jacket. I was so glad that what she had in her hand wasn't a sword after all. I was so glad she wasn't The Bogman. I let out a big breath.

"Anna!" I said. "What are you doing here? I thought we were meeting you back at the snow cave."

"Well, I was waiting there, but you guys took so long, I thought I'd come get you," she said. "What took you so long? I already did everything else I was supposed to do to get ready for the treasure."

"I got mixed up walking back," I said, feeling a little silly. "I wasn't paying attention and it started snowing harder and harder."

"Hey, wait a minute, guys. What treasure?" Gracey interrupted. "What do you mean, Anna, you're going to bury a treasure with that shovel?"

Anna and I looked at each other. We both knew right then that we had to tell Gracey.

"We're going to bury a secret treasure to trick Willy and Charlie. We want them to think it's a real treasure, like money, only we're just going to bury a bunch of gooey stuff," Anna said. "They've been teasing us a lot, so we're going to tease them."

"That's a good idea, I guess." Gracey said.

"Yeah, like trick or treat, only this is just the trick part," I said.

"Yeah, so they'll know it's not okay to pick on us. Come on," Anna said. "Let's go."

"Goody, goody!" Gracey said. "Let's go."

Gracey walked in front of us, and while Anna and I walked together I wanted to tell her how she had scared me, but I didn't want her to think I was silly. I mean, first I got mixed up walking home and then I thought she was The Bogman. Would she think I was stupid?

Well, she is my best friend. I guess I could tell her.

"Anna," I said, "Remember when we took that field trip and saw that video about The Bogman?"

"Yeah," she said. "That was so cool. I always wished we could have our own Bogman right here."

"Really?" I asked.

"Sure," she said. "We could make a big discovery and be famous. Everyone would want to come to our bog. I mean it practically is our bog. It's in back of our backyards. And we could give autographs."

"Well," I said, "It might sound great, but I thought you were

58

The Bogman back there. The snow was blowing everywhere. You know it's always windier near the bog because it's so open there, and for a couple minutes we were standing right near the bog and there were these loud noises coming from the ice. And I thought it could be The Bogman waking up. Then you came through the snow carrying the shovel, and I couldn't tell it was you. And the wind was shrieking and I thought it was The Bogman screaming. It was really very spooky."

"Bridget, you have a great imagination!" she said. "It must be all those books you read. You know, I only wish it were true what you thought you saw. We'd have our very own Bogman."

"I bet you wouldn't really want that once it happened," I said. "It was scary. At first all I could see was the ghost shape of someone coming at us in the snow. And then I thought it had a sword over its head and was coming to get us."

"Wow," she said. "That must have been pretty scary. Now I even have goosebumps. I'm glad it was just me after all!"

"Hey," Gracey said, stopping and looking back at us. "Is my doll-baby still okay in the snow cave?"

"She sure is," Anna said. "Do you want to go back right now to get her?"

"Well, if she's okay, then I'd really like to go with you and Bridget first," Gracey said. Then she whispered, "To bury the treasure, you know."

"Okay," said Anna. "I left the bucket of slop just off the trail up there. It was too heavy to carry. We'll get it, and then we'll bury it. We still have time before Willie and Charlie get back from karate."

CHAPTER
SIX

Burying
the Treasure

"Anna," I asked as we walked, "don't you think it's getting a bit too dark? Maybe we should wait until tomorrow morning to do this. It's still snowing kind of hard and I don't think it's going to stop. I saw big storm clouds."

"Oh, you're just shook up from The Bogman," Anna said. "Don't worry. I've been through these woods a million times. I know the way. Besides, I found my way from the snow cave, didn't I?"

I had to admit she was right.

"Plus, you know Willie and Charlie already saw the note," Anna said. "And they'll be out looking for the treasure as soon as they get back from their karate class in Saranac Lake. So we have to bury it now before it's too late. Remember, we wrote 'Saturday' on the treasure map, so they're expecting it to be there today."

"Okay," I said.

We walked some more, and then found the pail full of old food that my mother had been saving for the compost pile. Anna had put it down next to a big tree in plain sight. It looked pretty gross. There were brown banana peels and mushy coffee grounds and moldy orange rinds and slimy spaghetti. Anna had already poured the sour milk over everything, so it smelled awful. It was perfect!

I carried the pail by the handle, and we walked toward the bunch of birch trees where we would bury it. Anna said she had tied yarn around four other trees leading to the spot, the same as we had marked on the map. The yarn was bright orange, so the boys would be sure to see it. Anna's yarn was from her mother's knitting basket. Her mom makes a lot of sweaters and mittens and stuff like that. She sells them at craft fairs.

Finally, we reached the secret spot. Gracey sat down in the snow while Anna and I got ready to go to work. We picked a spot right near a big birch tree and cleared all the snow away first. Then we took turns digging. It was really hard because the ground was frozen. It took a lot longer than we thought.

"I want something to do, too," Gracey said. So we told her she could be the lookout person, and she could watch to make sure Willie and Charlie were nowhere in sight while we were digging.

When the hole looked pretty big, we tried to fit the pail into it. But the hole still wasn't deep enough. My arms hurt from digging. So then Anna dug some more. It was getting hard to see because it was getting darker. The hole still wasn't big enough, though, so we rested against the trees for a little while.

Gracey said she was tired of being on the lookout, and she was getting cold. She wanted to go home.

"But we're almost done," Anna said.

"I want to go home," Gracey said. "I want to get my doll-baby Patty and go home and have some hot chocolate and wait for Peter to come over."

Anna and I looked at each other.

"I'm not going," Anna said. "I want to finish burying this, and then I want to hide behind that little hill over there. I can see this spot just perfect from there. I want to see Willie and Charlie's faces when they find this pail. I want to hear every word they say, too!"

Gracey started crying.

Uh oh.

I stood up, and brushed the snow from my jacket and pants.

"Bridget, will you take me home?" she said, wiping her nose with the back of her mitten. "And we can stop in the snow cave and get Lester and Patty?"

I looked at Anna.

"Go ahead," she said. "I can finish by myself."

She pulled a piece of an old sheet out of her coat pocket.

"Once I fit the pail into the hole, I'm going to cover it with this sheet. It's from the old scraps my mother keeps for dusting and stuff like that. You see, once Willie and Charlie get all the snow off and start digging with their hands, they'll be so excited, they'll just pull off the sheet as soon as they see the pail and dig their hands inside expecting money!" Anna said.

"And they'll never know I'm going to be there the whole time watching. And then when I get home I'll tell you guys everything they say, and then on Monday I'll tell everyone on the bus. And then I'll tell the whole class!"

She smiled. Her braces sparkled.

"They won't like being made fun of. And then they'll know how it feels to be called Steel. And I'll bet they won't call you Seal anymore either!"

"That would be great," I said.

"Okay, let's make this like a real secret thing," Anna said. "We'll make a pledge, like they do in clubs."

She took my hand, and Gracey's hand, and Gracey took my other hand. We formed a small circle around the hole in the ground.

"We are now called the Secret Spooky Snow Club," Anna said. "I think that's a good name because we have a secret snow cave, and secret treasure, and a secret plan. And we do spooky stuff in the snow."

She looked at me and winked. I knew she was talking about The Bogman.

"Yeah, like our trick on Willie and Charlie is spooky," Gracey said.

"Okay, everyone say 'I promise to keep all our secrets.'"

"I promise to keep all our secrets," I said.

"I promise to keep all our secrets," Gracey said. "But wait, there's one more secret. Bridget and I found the pitcher plants near the bog. And we want to keep that secret, too, because we don't want anyone to pick them."

"Okay, it's a deal," said Anna. "Now everybody squeeze each others' hands, and say all at the same time, 'I swear to keep the secrets of the Secret Spooky Snow Club. And I will not ever pick on anyone who has braces or wears snowpants.'"

We all repeated what she said.

"What about glasses?" Gracey asked.

"What do you mean?" I asked.

"Well, this girl in my class has to wear glasses and some people teased her about that and the teacher said that wasn't very nice. I don't think we should ever pick on anyone with glasses, either."

So we added that to our pledge.

"What about a secret password?" I asked. "Shouldn't we have one for our club?"

"Good idea," Anna said. "Let's see...how about snow angel?"

We all agreed, and then Gracey and I headed back to the snow cave.

CHAPTER
SEVEN

The Woods at Night

This time I paid very close attention to where I was walking. First I saw a couple of the trees where Anna had tied yarn, so I knew I was heading the right way. But I had to admit, it had taken a lot longer than I thought to dig that hole, and now the sky was darker than before.

I walked very carefully, watching everything around me so I would be sure of the way. When you're in the woods a lot, you can notice different things about trees, like thick bark, or odd-shaped branches or big knots.

Finally, I saw a third tree with yarn on it, but that made me realize that I missed a turn in the path. There were four trees with yarn on them, and I knew two of the trees were in a different direction from the snow cave because we didn't want Willie and Charlie to find our secret hideout.

So I told Gracey we had to turn around, and we started walking back the way we had come. I knew the right path wasn't very far away, but it was hard to see everything clearly because now we were walking in a different direction. We were facing the wind again and it was blowing the snow around. I saw an opening in the woods and thought it looked like the right path, so we turned that way.

I held Gracey's hand and we sang a couple of songs while we walked through the woods. She has the same teacher I did in kindergarten, Mrs. Nason, so we both know a lot of the same songs. As I sang, I thought that my voice sounded too small for the wind. The wind kept lifting up, higher and higher above our faces. It seemed like the sky got lower and the wind got higher. Without any leaves to make the wind softer, like in summer, the wind didn't whisper the way I love it to. It just kept getting louder. It sounded like a mad wind.

I never understood why people say the wind whistles when it's cold out. Whistling is a cheerful thing, like my dad does when he's piling wood on a nice, cool day. The noise of a cold wind is different, especially at night. It's like holding your mouth open in the shape of a capital letter O and then blowing out the word "WHO" very slowly for a really long time. It didn't sound cheerful. It sounded spooky, like it had back at the bog. I shivered thinking about The Bogman again.

Gracey tugged at my arm.

"I'm tired, Bridget," she said. "And I'm cold."

She held up her mittens for me to see. They were the wool mittens that her mother had made, and they were kind of wet and soggy now.

I took her mittens off and unzipped my jacket and put her hands under my armpits. That's the warm spot. I know because that's where I snuggle with my mom.

After that I gave her my mittens and stuck my hands in my jacket pockets.

"I think we're almost there," I said.

We walked some more, but I noticed that there were a lot of low branches that I had to keep pushing out of the way. I didn't remember our path having that many branches. We should have been out to the big field behind our house by now.

I looked up, and through the high branches of the trees I could

see that the sky was dark and cloudy. I started thinking the branches looked like big, skinny hands reaching out to grab us. I shook my head to try to shake the thought out. It was too scary.

It was still snowing. The clouds were moving fast, and when one big one moved I saw that the moon had been behind it. It was a full moon. I didn't know if the moon was out early tonight, or if it was a lot later than I thought. I just hoped that at least the moon would stay out of the clouds, because it was a nice moon and it helped me to see.

Even though nothing that I could see looked familiar.

I wondered if we were lost.

I remember my father always told me "If you ever get lost, Bridget, stay right where you are." But did he mean the place where you were when you got lost—even if it was out in the cold wind—or someplace safe, like the snow cave?

I really didn't think we could be that far from the snow cave, so I decided to walk some more. It couldn't be far now. I'd probably just gone around the long way. We walked for a while longer, and then one of the branches scratched my face. Just then the moon was covered with clouds and everything got dark again. I felt a empty spot in my stomach. I was worried.

Since I couldn't see very well, and my face was stinging, we stopped to lean against a tree to rest. This one was a cedar tree. I could tell by the sweet smell; Mom puts cedar chips in our closet to keep moths away from our clothes. The closet smells good that way.

"I have some cookie chunks left," Gracey said. She pulled them out of her pocket. I tried not to think about the strawberry swirl ice cream I had wanted earlier. I was starving. Anyway, it was too cold for ice cream now. And I was hungrier than that. I wanted french fries and hot chocolate. I wanted a triple-cheese pizza.

I realized that if I was lost, everyone would be mad at me. Even if The Bogman didn't get us, I'd never get a babysitting job now.

After we ate the rest of the cookie chunks, the moon came out from behind the clouds again and we tried to walk a little more. The bad part about the moon being out was that it was so bright that it made long, scary shadows from every tree, so it looked like there were twice as many of them. The shadows were like tree ghosts, I thought, but that made me feel like screaming.

And I knew that even without the shadows, the woods were getting thicker, so then I knew for sure that I was lost now. We should have been to the field long ago. We never walked this deep into the woods before.

Pretty soon, I couldn't see the moon any more because of all the trees. I felt so scared. I didn't know what to do. I thought that now was the time to stay right where we were. Because we were lost for sure.

"We're gonna' stop again, Gracey," I said. "It's kind of hard to see. Let's rest a bit."

She leaned against me.

"I want to go home," she said. Her voice was low. I knew she was really tired.

I didn't feel very good about being lost. I felt hot tears fill my

75

eyes. I didn't know what else to do except just stop right here. My brain felt kind of heavy trying to think of anything else right now except stopping. Because this is the place where we were lost. And that's what my dad always said to do. Stop when you're lost.

My skin felt tingly, like it knew I was scared. It was really quiet out here in the woods in the dark. I hoped I wouldn't hear any animal noises. I felt very, very small and the woods seemed very, very big. Everywhere I looked there was just the black outline of trees and more trees. And I didn't like not knowing what was behind them.

My hands were cold from having to take them out of my coat pockets too much to push branches out of the way. I stuck them back into my pockets to warm them up.

Way down in the corner of my right pocket, where my hand was, I could feel my Swiss Army knife. And then I had an idea!

CHAPTER
EIGHT

Building a Shelter

"Gracey, I'm going to make us a little shelter," I said. "We can huddle under that. It will be another secret place for our club, okay?"

"Okay," she said. "I want to rest. I want Patty."

I started cutting some of the little branches with my knife, just like I had when we made our cave last summer. There were no cliffs or boulders around to make a great cave like ours, but I found one rock that was kind of big and I piled some long boughs from pine trees against it, leaving enough room between the rock and the branches for Gracey and I to sit down. At least it would keep the snow and the wind off us for awhile.

While I worked, I kept telling myself that we would be okay, because someone would find us. All the grown-ups knew how to get around the woods in back of our house. And they'd have flashlights. And the moon would help them see our tracks. And Anna must be home by now to get help.

I had to keep telling myself the good things, just like that time I slept over at Anna's and I was scared, because right now I felt like just curling up and crying. I wished I was safe in bed like I had been that night, or safe in my mother's snowplow riding up high in all this snow. Then I wouldn't be scared. One time she let me ride with her in the snowplow at night. The snowplow is so high up I had to use a little ladder just to reach the bottom step. And my mom had to help push me in so I could reach the seat after that. But once I was up there in that big seat, I could see everything. It was like we had our own kingdom out there on the roads, late at night when most everyone else was already sleeping. I felt like a princess of the snow.

I liked remembering that feeling. It's good to remember good things like that when you're afraid. It makes less room for scary thoughts.

It took me a long time to cut the pine boughs. When I had enough, I called Gracey and we huddled together underneath the branches. They smelled good. I pulled some more of them around the sides of us. The woods didn't seem quite so big now that we were in a little space. It was so quiet, I could hear the heavy snow land softly on the branches. As I listened, I thought it made the same sound the foam makes at the ocean after the waves have gone back out to sea, and the foam just settles into the sand. It was a nice gentle sound.

I put my arm around Gracey, and then she started crying.

"I want to go home. I want my mommy and daddy," she said. "And my friend Peter will think I forgot him," she said.

I felt my eyes fill up with tears. They were hot. I wiped them away. I wished I had Lester with me.

"Are you crying, too?" Gracey asked.

"Yeah," I said. "My mom said sometimes it's good to cry, though. It makes you feel better sometimes because it washes a lot of worry away."

"Do you think those angel guards will hear us crying and come help us?" Gracey asked.

"Oh, I think those guardian angels will hear us. You know, that's a good thought, Gracey," I said. "Maybe we should keep talking, too, and then they'll know where we are and they can send someone to find us."

I knew that no matter what, we couldn't fall asleep, so I thought the talking would also help us stay awake. My dad told me it's dangerous to fall asleep in the woods in the cold because you could freeze. I cuddled up closer to Gracey.

"Just think, everyone will be happy to see us when they find us. And we'll be safe in our houses again," I said.

"But you have two houses now, don't you?" Gracey asked.

I felt a little lump in my throat, wondering if my mom or dad even knew yet that I was lost. I missed both of them so much right now. I heard an owl call out in the woods. I wondered if it ever scared itself, making noises at night.

"I guess I do have two houses," I said. "But I always have a place to go. I get to have two bedrooms, and two bikes, and two of everything."

"Sometime can I go to your dad's house with you and have him tell me those stories about the signs while he drives us?" Gracey asked.

"Sure!" I said. "That's a great idea. Hey, let's make up some stories of our own right now about signs."

"But I can't read all the way yet. I don't know what signs say," Gracey said.

"Okay, I'll tell you one. I saw a sign last week that I'd never seen before. I was going to a new friend's house after school and her mom took us down some roads I've never been on. And I saw this sign that said FROST HEAVES and I've been thinking about it a lot. What do you think that could mean?"

Gracey thought for a minute. Then she sat up.

"Well, it could be something about Jack Frost!" she said. "You know, he's the guy that always comes and puts the frost on everything right before it starts to snow all the time. My teacher told us a poem about him."

"Yeah!" I said, clapping my hands in excitement. "I never thought of that. Of course, Jack Frost. And you know, heave is another word for barf, or throw up. I heard Willie say one day that he thought he was going to heave after Mr. Bullock hit a really big bump in the road on the bus! He said his stomach went up really high and he could feel his pancakes coming back up!"

"Oh," said Gracey, "I'm REALLY glad he didn't throw up on the bus."

"Me, too!" I said. "But you see, the sign FROST HEAVES could mean, watch out, Jack Frost is going to throw up!" I said.

We laughed a long time thinking about that.

Then Gracey said that she knew of one sign that didn't have any words. It showed a deer on its two hind legs, and the two front legs were raised up in the air.

"My mom told me it means to watch out because it's a spot where deer run across the road," Gracey said. "But you know, I always thought it looked more like a deer that was dancing. Now that you told me how signs have stories, I think that sign really means to watch out, because there's DEER DANCING up ahead!"

"I really like that idea," I said. "You know, I bet that deer can dance. Why not? Wait until I tell my dad about that sign. He'll really like that, Gracey."

I put my arm around her, because I know how good that feels when you're sad, and it kept me from feeling alone and scared, too.

"Are you warm enough?" I asked.

"I'm a little cold," Gracey said.

"Me, too," I said. I sure did hate to admit it, but I was really, really glad that my mother made me wear my snowpants today. I would have been freezing by now.

"Maybe we should go outside our little shelter here and dance around a bit, you know, like the deer. That would keep us warm," I said.

"Okay," Gracey said.

"Gracey," I said, "When we get home, you can have my second-best doll to keep forever, because you're so brave."

She smiled at me.

We stepped outside the little shelter. The moon was really bright, and for a minute I forgot we were lost because the forest was so pretty. All the branches on the trees were covered with snow, even the little ones, and it made it look as if every one had its own little blanket. Then I felt scared inside, thinking about how we might have to stay in the woods all night.

"Come on, let's dance," I said, and we shook all over, lifting our legs up and shaking our arms, singing parts of songs really loud. Then we got tired again.

Gracey looked up at the sky. "The moon is like a friend," she said.

"You know, when you were a baby, 'moon' is one of the first words you ever said," I told her. "I remember. You were always pointing up and saying 'moon, moon.'"

Gracey giggled. We just stood there together, looking at the moon. Then I felt Gracey tugging at my sleeve. "Look," she whispered, "Over there."

CHAPTER
NINE

Out of the Woods

I turned, and there in the woods was a mother deer and her fawn, just watching us. Gracey and I stood still, just like the animals did. Their fur looked sort of like brown velvet in the snow, and their eyes were the same color as the cattails that grow in the swamps. The doe's long neck was near the fawn to protect it, I think.

I suddenly felt warmer inside, because I just felt that somehow they were watching over us, too.

"They're so pretty," Gracey whispered. "I think they're our friends. They're not scared."

"I guess they feel safe with us," I said.

As we looked at the deer, I noticed that beyond them there seemed to be a faint, wide light. I wondered if it could be a house. It must be something.

"Gracey," I said, "Let's walk a little bit more. The moon is out again, it can help us to see. I think I see something up ahead."

She took my hand. As we started walking, the deer ran into the woods, and we could see their white tails behind them as they ran.

"Hey, they're dancing!" Gracey said. "Bye-bye, deer," she said, waving her other hand.

"Bye," I said.

We walked slowly toward the open area. Our feet were dragging, because we were still tired. But I was sure this was the right thing to do because if it was lighter up ahead it had to mean something. It could be somebody's backyard and there could be light from their house shining out. I'd even be happy to see Willie and

Charlie's house. I wondered if they'd ever found the treasure.

As we came closer and closer to the light, there were fewer trees and I could see an open area ahead. Finally, I pushed aside some bushes, and we practically tumbled down a small hill as we came out of the woods.

"It's the road, Gracey! The road!" I said.

I pulled her down the bank with me, and I told her that we'd wait right there, because someone would be sure to drive by and see us. This was a lot better than waiting in the dark woods. I didn't even mind that it was still snowing so much. At least it felt safer out here. It was brighter than where we were before, because there were no trees. The moon's light was much brighter in the open, and that's what I had seen.

I wanted us to sit somewhere so somebody driving by would see us. I looked around, and put my hands over my eyes to block the snow so at least I could see straight ahead, even if it was snowing too hard for me to look straight up. I saw a metal pole on the side of the road with piles of snow around it, and decided we should sit on top of the snowbank and rest against the pole. Any driver would be sure to notice a pole.

I pulled Gracey onto my lap. I was glad her snowsuit was bright pink.

"Someone will see us now," I said.

"Oh, good," she said, and she cuddled on my lap. Just before she fell asleep, she told me she thought maybe the guard angels heard

90

us talking after all and they sent the deer to lead us to the road.

I rocked her sideways while she slept on my lap. My eyes felt really heavy as I listened to her breathing. In and out. In and out. I didn't want to fall asleep though. Not yet. I had to stay awake for when a car came by.

I was really glad we were out of the woods.

I watched the road for a really long time and then I made myself start thinking about food again so I could stay awake. I thought about a big fat cheeseburger. I thought about my favorite place to eat pizza. I thought about a hot fudge sundae. I thought about strawberry licorice, that twisted kind. I figured I could eat the jumbo sized bag all by myself, just sitting here.

And then I thought about how, once I got home, I was going to stay in bed for three days at me and my mom's house and just read and sleep. Nothing else. Except maybe eat food brought to me on trays. And then I would spend three days at me and my dad's house and do the same thing. I thought that bed seemed like the best place in the world right now. And I thought that both my homes were a lot nicer places than the woods at night. I'd rather read about stuff like that than actually be there.

I stared out at the road some more, and the falling snow made me feel sleepy. I tried to count the flakes, but that made me sleepier. I thought I could see a yellow dot far away, and I wondered if it was the moon or I was starting to dream like sometimes you do when you're still about half awake. Then the dot got a little brighter. A yellow dot...a big yellow dot... Hey, it was a yellow DOT! It was my mother's DOT snowplow coming down the road. Oh, I hoped I wasn't starting to dream.

I struggled to sit up, but I couldn't with Gracey on my lap. So I waved my arms. It was the snowplow!

Beep! Beep! Beep!

The truck barely stopped before my mom was jumping down from the cab and running toward us. Then, from around the other side of the big yellow truck came my dad! It was my mom and dad in the snowplow together again!

Anna and her mom and dad pulled up right behind the snowplow in their car, and Willie and Charlie hopped out of the back seat. I thought I must be seeing things.

"BRIDGET!" Mom called, crying, as she ran up to me and hugged me and Gracey so hard my eyelids got squished. "GRACEY!" she said. And then Anna and her mom and dad pulled Gracey out from between us and kept hugging her, and then me.

A lot of people were crying.

Gracey was still half asleep and she was trying to tell everyone about the deer and the guard angels and Jack Frost barfing.

Anna said that she had waited for Willie and Charlie to come find the treasure, and sure enough, they came with their big flashlights and they dug up the bucket and got all gooey and it was the funniest thing she'd ever seen. But then they saw her watching them and they chased her all the way back to her house. Her mother was standing on the porch, she said, wondering where Gracey and I were.

"That's when I realized you guys were lost," Anna said. She wiped her eyes and her voice shook a little. Then she took a deep breath.

"And you know what? Willie and Charlie used their flashlights and they helped us all look for you guys. They weren't even mad anymore about the buried treasure trick."

I looked over at Willie and Charlie. They were next to the big plow, just smiling at us. I really think they were glad to see us.

"We couldn't see much in the woods," Anna's mom said, "because the wind had blown over your footprints and it was snowing so hard. So we went back home and I called your mom and dad."

I looked at my mom.

"I should have known you'd find us in your snowplow," I said, and everyone laughed.

I decided right then that I loved her snowplow more than ever. It was the biggest, most beautiful thing in the world.

"Well, sometime I'll give you another ride, Bridget," she said. "I'd much rather have you up there with me than out in the woods!"

As I hugged my mom, I looked over her shoulder and there was my dad, waiting for a hug, holding Lester in one hand, and Patty in the other. Gracey shrieked, and then I did, too.

He gave Patty to Gracey and kissed her on the head, and then he bent down and hugged me really hard. It was one of his big bear hugs.

"Your mom and I looked for you in the woods, too, for quite a while, as soon as we got here," he said. "First I found Lester and Gracey's doll in the snow cave. Anna showed me where it was, as long as I promised not to tell Willie and Charlie."

"Don't worry, he didn't tell us." Willie said. "But I bet we can find it! No problem."

"Yeah, we can find it!" Charlie said.

Anna just smiled at them. It was a big fat smile. She didn't even try to hide her braces.

"We looked all around the snow cave, and then at the bog," my dad said. "We saw some footprints in the woods, but we couldn't find any in the open areas because the wind blew the snow over them and covered them. We knew you must have gotten off the path because we couldn't find any footprints there. The last ones we saw seemed to be heading toward the road. So we decided we'd try the road on the far side of the field, thinking maybe that's where you headed."

He stopped talking then and took a big breath.

"We've been driving up and down the road real slow, beeping and hollering out your names," he said.

Then he stopped talking.

I could hear my dad gulp real hard then.

"We were hoping that you'd find your way to the road," he said.

Then I saw some tears in my father's eyes, and he made another gulp and it made a big noise in his neck. Then he hugged me again so tightly that I thought I'd lose my oxygen like The Bogman! Boy, was I glad to be safe!

Then my dad picked me up and he turned me toward the metal pole I had been leaning against. He took out a flashlight from his pocket, and pointed it up in the swirling snow.

"I want you to see something," he said.

I followed the beam of the flashlight. Way at the top of the metal pole was a road sign. It said....SOFT SHOULDERS.

My dad was smiling as wide as a river. It made his mustache tickle my face.

Maybe he didn't make those stories up after all.

About the Author

Liza Frenette lived in the Adirondack Mountains for thirty years, where she had many adventures in the woods. She has worked as a writer for newspapers, magazines, and newsletters. After graduating from Morrisville College with an associate's degree in journalism, she worked for the *Tupper Lake Free Press,* and then the *Adirondack Daily Enterprise* and the *Press Republican,* where she won several United Press International and Associated Press awards. She also wrote freelance for *Adirondack Life Magazine.* Then she moved out of the woods to write about the magazine industry for *FOLIO: Magazine* in Fairfield County, Connecticut. From there she moved to Albany, New York to return to college.

At the State University of New York at Albany she earned a bachelor's degree in English with a journalism minor, and then a master's degree in English in the creative writing program. Two of her short stories have been published in the anthology, *The Little Magazine.*

Because she enjoyed going back to school so much, she decided to specialize in writing about higher education for a career. She has been doing so ever since, in Albany, where she lives with her daughter Jasmine, who has been a beacon throughout many of the author's life changes, and provided some changes of her own! Liza continues to freelance write about many subjects and different people, and as you can see by this book, she writes fiction as well, something she has loved to do since she was the age of the older girls in this story. She loves the spirituality of the many wonderful paths she's found in the woods around Albany for walking and cross-country skiing. The Albany area is a great midway point between two of her favorite places, the Adirondack Mountains and Cape Cod, both of which she visits regularly for nourishment. This is her first published book, and she is happy to have it so beautifully illustrated by her first cousin, Jane Gillis.

About the Illustrator

Jane Gillis was born and raised in the Tip Top town of Tupper Lake, where she played in the woods, skied, canoed, and hiked with her many cousins and siblings. The North Country Girl Scout Camp on Lake Clear found Jane and her sisters there for many summers, where they got their first overnight canoeing and Adirondack High Peaks experiences. Later, in high school, Jane, her sister Barbara, cousins, and friends spent weekends in the woods climbing the High Peaks and canoeing down rivers, when they weren't working in the family business, The Market Place.

Jane always loved drawing as much as the outdoors, and pursued an art career at North Country Community College, SUNY College at Buffalo, and the Lake Placid School of Art. After graduating, Jane did freelance work in calligraphy and design, costumes for summer theatre and "Cold River," an Adirondack adventure film, as well as illustrations for the W. Alton Jones Cell Science Center in Lake Placid. Jane and her friends still hiked, canoed, skied, and climbed in the High Peaks until she moved to Maine in 1982 to pursue a career in medical illustration in the Medical Media Department of the Department of Veterans Affairs in Togus, Maine. Much to her son's Eliot's consternation, she reached 42 of the 46 High Peaks, but hasn't yet finished them!

Jane, her husband David, and their son moved to Marin County just outside of San Francisco in 1992 where they discovered the beautiful Mount Tamalpais and her wonderful trails and hiking groups. In 1995 the family moved to Medford, Oregon, where they now reside, surrounded by the Rogue River National Forest. Through all of her travels around the world, and all of the beautiful places she has called home, the Adirondacks continue to be a place of inspiration and spiritual renewal for the artist.